P9-BYW-060

Written by
Diane McAffee

Illustrated by
Guy Francis

Bookcraft
Salt Lake City, Utah

ISBN 1-57008-533-1

First Printing, 1998

Printed in the United States of America

Nicholas Pickett liked to play soccer, eat peanut butter and jelly sandwiches, tease his sister, Sara, and watch cartoons. He did not like to take out the garbage, go to bed, do homework, or take a bath.

But all that changed one Tuesday night when Nicholas didn't get his own way. The whole affair began when Mother told Nicholas that he could have chocolate ice cream after he finished his dinner.

Nicholas loved chocolate ice cream. In fact, it was his favorite thing in the whole world. No one has ever loved anything more than Nicholas loved chocolate ice cream.

When Mother went to the freezer, she found that the chocolate ice cream was gone. She said, "I'm so sorry, Nicholas. It looks like someone ate all the chocolate. How about strawberry tonight, and then when I go to the store I will get a carton of chocolate just for you." But instead of eating strawberry ice cream Nicholas Pickett began his Amazing, Incredible Sulk.

It started with a pouty face. "I want chocolate ice cream, and I want it now!" Nicholas said. "Well, we don't have any," said Mom, "so you can have strawberry, or you will just have to go without." The pout deepened into a full frown.

Nicholas slumped down in his chair and said, "I'm not moving until I get my ice cream." Mom sighed, and said, "I told you I was sorry, Nicholas. I thought we had chocolate ice cream left. But if you want, you can sit here until Saturday. That's when I shop next."

When Dad came home from work, he and Mom did the dishes, and Sara watched her and Nicholas's favorite TV show. But Nicholas sat and sulked. When it was time for bed Mom said, "Nicholas, why don't you go up to bed? You will feel better in the morning."

But Nicholas just frowned harder and said nothing. Mom went to bed and turned out the light on Nicholas. "What an Amazing, Incredible Sulk!" Mom said.

The next morning Nicholas was still frowning. Mother fixed pancakes and orange juice, but Nicholas was too busy sulking to eat. He sat and sulked all day long. Then he sulked all night.

When Dad came down to breakfast he said, “Nicholas, this has gone on for way too long! I want you to stop it right now!” But Nicholas just frowned. Sara said, “Nicholas, would you like to play soccer?” But Nicholas only frowned harder.

Even though it was only Thursday, Mother went to the store and bought chocolate ice cream. Lots of it. But Nicholas was sulking because he hadn’t gotten ice cream on Tuesday. He wouldn’t eat even one bite. “Can you believe this Amazing, Incredible Sulk?” asked Dad.

ICE CREAM

Mom and Dad took Nicholas to the doctor. The doctor looked in Nicholas's ears, listened to his heart, and thumped his knees. But Nicholas wouldn't open his mouth and say ahhh. The doctor thought very hard, scratched his head, and said, "It looks to me like Nicholas is sulking."

Mom and Dad took Nicholas to a psychiatrist. She asked Nicholas all sorts of questions, but he just sat and scowled. Finally the psychiatrist said, "Nicholas is suffering from a very serious case of sulkitis. That will be two hundred dollars, please."

Grandma came for a visit, and after looking at Nicholas she said, "Just ignore him. He will eventually get over it." Nicholas sat and sulked for three more weeks. "What an Amazing, Incredible Sulk!" Grandma said. But everyone took Grandma's advice and just ignored Nicholas. Nicholas only sulked harder.

Sulkitis
$200.00

One day Mother said to Dad, “Dear, Nicholas is in the way. Would you please move him over to the corner?” So Dad set Nicholas in the corner. “He needs to be dusted,” Dad said. So Sara got the job of dusting Nicholas off every other day. “Do you think he needs to be watered too?” she asked. Dad said no.

During the winter the family found that Nicholas made a great coatrack. They hung their hats on his ears and kept their boots in his lap. And still Nicholas sulked.

After a few years the family needed a nicknack cupboard. They moved Nicholas to the living room, where everyone could see Mother's collection of butter dishes. "What an interesting nicknack shelf!" all the ladies said.

Eventually Sara got married, and Mom and Dad moved into a condominium, but Nicholas refused to move. He was all grown up now, and his beard was the only thing that ever changed—and it grew ever so slowly. He stayed in the house because the family moving in needed a place to hang tools. Nicholas was perfect. And still he frowned. "This is an Amazing, Incredible Sulk!" said the new family.

Years and years went by. During those years Nicholas took turns serving as a bookcase, a toy box, a linen cupboard, and a clothesline for the families who lived in the house. One family even sat him in front of the window, with azaleas on his head so the plants could get some sun.

Finally a family moved in who did not need Nicholas to hold anything. “Take him out to the back porch,” the mother said. Nicholas sulked all through the summer and fall. He frowned through the winter, and when spring came a bird made a nest in his beard and a squirrel slept on his shoulder. “Have you ever seen someone in such an Amazing, Incredible Sulk?” people asked.

The Goodwill truck picked Nicholas up when he was put out with the rest of the old, useless, and broken things no one needed. A farmer bought Nicholas from Goodwill for $4.59. "Just what I need," he said.

The farmer attached a pointer to the top of Nicholas's head and set him on the top of the barn. "What a fine weather vane!" exclaimed the farmer.

W
N
S
E

No one knows exactly how long Nicholas sat on the top of the barn, but a very big windstorm finally blew him down. The farmer set him out in the cornfield to scare away the crows. And still Nicholas frowned. No one in the world had ever had such an Amazing, Incredible Sulk!

One day in early spring Nicholas's sister, Sara, walked out into the field with her granddaughter, Stacey. Stacey had a frown on her face that made her look very much like her great-uncle Nicholas. "See, honey?" Grandmother Sara said. "If you don't stop pouting you will end up looking just like Uncle Nicholas."

Stacey stared at Uncle Nicholas, whose face had hardened into a permanent frown. "Uncle Nicholas," she asked, "what are you sulking about?"

Nicholas Pickett sat up straight. He thought and thought. He thought so hard he turned bright red. But he could not remember, for the life of him, what he was sulking about. "I can't remember," he sheepishly admitted.

"Well, Uncle Nicholas, isn't it silly to sulk, when you don't even know what you're sulking about?" Nicholas stretched his face this way and that. He grimaced and growled, and finally, with a crack and a creak, one corner of his mouth turned up, and he smiled for the first time in years and years and years. "I guess so," he admitted.

“I’ll stop sulking if you will,” said Stacey. She reached out and took Nicholas’s hand. “Why don’t you come home with us?” So Nicholas Pickett ended his Amazing, Incredible Sulk. Grandma had been right. Eventually Nicholas got over it.